Barbie in A CHRISTMAS CAROL

A Junior Novelization

Adapted by Holly Kowitt
Based on the original screenplay
by Elise Allen
Illustrations by Rainmaker Entertainment

SCHOLASTIC INC.

New York   Toronto   London   Auckland   Sydney
Mexico City   New Delhi   Hong Kong   Buenos Aires

Special Thanks to Rob Hudnut, Cort Lane, Carrie Wilksen, Vicki Jaeger, Monica Okazaki, Jennifer Twiner McCarron, Anita Lee, Pat Link, Pam Prostarr, Elizabeth Gonzales, Shaun Martens, and David Dick

ISBN-13: 978-0-545-10481-4
ISBN-10: 0-545-10481-5

12 11 10 9 8 7 6 5 4 3 2 1   8 9 10 11 12/0

Printed in the U.S.A.
First printing, October 2008

Introduction

Barbie took one last look at herself in the mirror. Her silver evening dress with the giant bow looked stunning. Sparkly earrings glittered against her long blond hair.

She ran into the hall to find her sister. "Kelly," she shouted, "we have to go!" Why did little sisters always pick the worst time to disappear? Barbie darted back into her room to grab her purse. As she passed the mirror, she noticed something move in the reflection.

Behind the beanbag chair, a blond head

was sticking out. Barbie rolled her eyes, but she couldn't help smiling. She reached over the beanbag and tickled her sister. Kelly shrieked.

"Tell me you haven't been in my room this whole time!" said Barbie.

Her sister got up and smoothed out her party dress. It was green and had satin trimming and silvery snowflakes embroidered along the bottom. She wore a green headband and green shoes that matched the dress perfectly.

"The Charity Christmas Ball starts in five minutes," said Barbie. "Our friends and family are already there. Come on!"

Kelly frowned and sank into the beanbag chair, folding her arms.

"Looks like someone's got the Christmas spirit," joked Barbie.

"I don't want to go to the ball," said Kelly, pouting. "I want to do what we do every Christmas Eve. I want to stay home, make cookies, drink cider, and sing carols! That's what we do, and I'm staying here until we do it!"

Barbie sighed. The ball raised money for a hospital, and their friends and family

were all going. She explained to Kelly it was for a really good cause.

"I *hate* Christmas," Kelly blurted out.

Barbie looked at her sister closely. Kelly's eyes were puffy, and her arms were crossed. Barbie put down her purse.

"You know what?" said Barbie. "I think it's okay if we run a little late." She reached up to a high bookcase and handed Kelly a beautiful old snow globe.

Kelly took the globe carefully. "You said I wasn't allowed to touch this," she said. Through the glass, they could see a Victorian town with three female figures. One was in white, one in green, and one in red.

"There's a story behind this snow globe," said Barbie. "A story about the beauty of Christmas, and how one girl discovered it many, many years ago . . ."

As she spoke, she wound a key on the bottom of the snow globe. A music box played "O Christmas Tree." They looked deeply into the glass, and the village came alive.

Chapter 1

Snow was coming down hard outside the Gadshill Theatre. Located in the bustling city of Victorian London, the building was packed for a Saturday matinee. Inside, the audience watched a beautiful girl sing in front of a blazing Christmas tree. When she finished, they broke into wild applause. Someone handed her a bouquet of flowers.

"That's Eden Starling," said Barbie. "She was the most famous singing star in

Victorian England. She was beautiful, talented . . . and incredibly full of herself. And that's her cat, Chuzzlewit."

The moment Eden left the stage, she tossed her bouquet off to the side. The flowers hit the keyboard of a harpsichord where a Persian cat was sleeping. The harpsichord blared loudly and the cat fell to the ground.

"Rowr!" he meowed angrily. Embarrassed, he quickly looked around to see if anyone saw him fall. Then without missing a beat, he fell into step right behind Eden, who scooped him up into her arms.

"I hate Christmas," Eden said grouchily.

❄ ❄ ❄

"Hey! That's what I said," Kelly pointed out.

"*Really?*" smiled Barbie. "Total coincidence."

❄ ❄ ❄

Eden put Chuzzlewit down, and he followed her backstage. On the way, she passed a number of props for the stage troupe —

juggling pins, a trapeze, and a cage of doves.

"I'm tired of singing carols every year," said Eden. "I perform opera, Chuzzlewit, *opera!*" But Chuzzlewit was far more interested in the doves. He pawed at the cage, and the birds fluttered wildly about. Eden stopped abruptly in her tracks, causing Chuzzlewit to bump right into her.

"*Where* are my tea and crumpets?!" demanded Eden. "There's *supposed* to be a tray! Where's Catherine? *Catherine!*"

Downstairs in the wardrobe area, Catherine Beadnell was sewing wings on a tiny felt angel. As the talented costume designer for the Gadshill, Catherine was adored by the troupe. While Eden had the power to hire and fire people, it was Catherine who truly ran the theatre. She and Eden were old friends, and Catherine was the only one who didn't tremble during Eden's terrible mood swings.

Catherine beamed at her creation, unaware of Eden. The backstage area was covered with gorgeous ornaments, wreaths, and decorations. The Gadshill troupe was happily trimming a large Christmas tree.

Ann and Nan were twin sisters, as well as talented singers and dancers. In matching glittery dresses, they took Catherine's ornaments and pirouetted to the tree. Maurice, the French clown, juggled glass balls while riding a unicycle.

Magnifico the Magnificent was a magician who wore a black cape and top hat. Also known as Freddy, he stood on a ladder and pulled a long strand of cranberries and popcorn from his pocket.

As he wrapped it around the tree, he smiled shyly at Catherine. He had a twinkle in his eye for her.

The troupe sang "Deck the Halls" while they decorated. Catherine hummed, and Ann and Nan danced over to Freddy. As they trimmed the tree, they whispered to him.

"So, when are you going . . ." Ann began.

". . . to ask her?" finished Nan.

Freddy was so startled, he nearly fell off the ladder. "Ask who?" he said. The twins danced off to get more ornaments, and Maurice rode by on his unicycle.

"Come now, Freddy, we all know you want to ask Catherine out on a date," whispered Maurice.

Freddy looked around, panicked. "She'll

hear you!" he whispered. He looked anxiously at Catherine, but she was still humming and sewing. When she looked up and saw Freddy, she waved. He was so flustered, he fell backward off the ladder. Strands of popcorn went flying everywhere.

"Whoooooa!" yelled Freddy.

Ann and Nan danced over to the tree and propped Freddy back up. Catherine giggled. Freddy gave her a blushing smile and went back to his popcorn strands.

"If you want to ask her out, do it before Christmas," whispered Maurice. "Otherwise, out of sight" — he snapped his fingers — "*pouf!* Out of mind."

Freddy looked worried. "You think so?"

Maurice nodded. "I *know* so," he said.

Freddy looked at Catherine and took a

deep breath. He kept pulling lengths of popcorn out of his pocket. "All right," he said. "Here I go. I'm going to ask —"

"*CATHERINE!*" screamed Eden.

Everyone jumped and saw Eden at the top of the stairs. She was carrying Chuzzlewit under one arm, and a plate of tea and crumpets in her other hand. Chuzzlewit stretched a furry paw out, trying to steal a crumpet, but couldn't quite reach. As Eden stormed downstairs, Ann, Nan, and Maurice froze in terror. Freddy kept pulling more and more popcorn strands out of his pocket, until at last there was no more popcorn left, and a pair of polka dot boxer shorts came out instead. He gasped with embarrassment and hastily stuffed them back into his pocket.

"Hello, Eden," Catherine said calmly. "Hello, Chuzzie!" she cooed to the cat. She leaned down to scratch him, but he turned up his nose.

"It's Chuzzlewit," said Eden irritably. "You know he hates 'Chuzzie.' Have you seen these?" She handed Catherine the plate, moving it even farther away from a disappointed Chuzzlewit.

"Oh, good," said Catherine. "I told the stagehands to get them for you."

"They have too much butter," Eden pouted. "What's going on here?" she asked, looking at the decorations. She placed the crumpets on a high shelf, now completely out of reach from Chuzzlewit.

"It's Christmas Eve!" said Catherine. "We wanted to celebrate before we go on holiday." The troupe looked proudly at the festive room.

"Holiday?! Who said anything about a holiday?" asked Eden, surprised. "There is no holiday. *No. Holiday.*"

Everyone was speechless.

Chapter 2

After a shocked silence, they all started talking at once.

"But it's . . ." Ann began.

"Christmas!" finished Nan.

"I'm aware it's Christmas," Eden said. "Which means there are only two weeks before you begin Eden Starling's new show. You should be begging to rehearse!"

Maurice shook his head. *"Non!"* he sputtered. *"C'est impossible!* This is an outrage!"

"We can't work on Christmas!" said Ann.

"People are coming," added Nan. "There's a turkey to stuff. And pies to bake!"

"You don't want to work on Christmas?" asked Eden. "Fine. Stay home." She folded her arms. "But if you do, don't bother coming back. *Ever!*"

Freddy got down on one knee and took off his hat. "Eden, please," he begged. As he removed his hat, a deck of cards poured out of his sleeve, and a dove flew out.

Chuzzlewit had almost made his way to the shelf with the crumpets on it when he spotted the dove. He licked his lips and leaped on the bird, but Freddy scooped it up just in the nick of time. However, Eden collided with Chuzzlewit mid-pounce. She felt her legs slide out from under her, and for several seconds, she and Chuzzlewit skittered wildly across the floor. The troupe held in their laughter as the two of them flailed helplessly.

When they got their footing back, Eden gave everyone an angry stare as she marched to her dressing room with Chuzzlewit in tow.

"Please talk to Eden," Maurice begged Catherine.

"You're the only one who could change her mind!" added Freddy.

Catherine got up and went to Eden's dressing room. Eden was brushing her hair at a fancy mirror; bouquets of flowers were everywhere. Chuzzlewit was curled on her lap.

"Seriously, Eden," Catherine started. "You're asking them to give up Christmas.

They have plans. *I* have plans."

"Bigger plans than my show?" asked Eden.

Eden got up, putting Chuzzlewit on the table. He admired himself in the mirror, then saw something in the reflection — a large tin of cookies. He licked his lips and leaped onto the tin, but the lid was shut tight. He struggled and fought, but couldn't pry it open. "Yes," said Catherine.

"I'm going home. My whole family will be there for Christmas. You know how important that is to me."

Eden sighed with frustration as she looked at her friend. "You know, I could have had any designer in London," said Eden. "But I insisted on you. And you don't care." She put her brush down. "I have to look out for myself. It's like Aunt Marie always said: 'In a selfish world, only the selfish succeed.'"

Catherine protested. "It's *not* a selfish world. And do you really want to take advice from Aunt Marie?"

Eden narrowed her eyes. "Don't *think* I haven't seen you sewing for another show. . . ."

"What?" said Catherine. "No, it's not what you —"

"Then prove it," said Eden. "Take down the tree, and work through Christmas. If anyone goes home, or says a word about Christmas, they're out. Including you."

As Eden spoke, she marched over to the door. "Does everyone understand?" she asked loudly. As she threw open the door, Freddy, Ann, Nan, and Maurice all toppled over. The group nodded sheepishly.

"Yes," Freddy said.

"We . . ." started Ann.

". . . understand," finished Nan.

Freddy gave Maurice an elbow jab. "*Oui, oui*," said the clown.

"It makes me sad to see you like this," said Catherine. "Merry Christmas, Eden."

Eden flounced back to her chair and picked up Chuzzlewit, who had finally gotten the top off the tin. She began to pet him, unaware that she just interrupted his snack. "Christmas," Eden muttered to herself. "Bah, humbug!"

✳ ❄ ✳

"Eden's mean," said Kelly, interrupting Barbie's story.

"You think so?" asked Barbie. "Wait till you hear what happens next . . ."

✳ ❄ ✳

In a fancy bedroom with a big canopy bed, Eden and Chuzzlewit were asleep in matching pink eye masks. They awoke up to a loud clanking noise, and at the foot of the bed stood an older woman wrapped in golden chains.

"Aunt Marie?" Eden gasped.

"Yes, my darling," the stately woman said dramatically, "it is I." As she floated closer, the chains got caught on a hat rack and pulled her down with a giant *CRASH*!

"Whoa!" she said.

Eden and Chuzzlewit looked at each other, and rushed to the foot of the bed. Aunt Marie was hopelessly tangled up in a pile of chains and hats.

"Blast and blunderbuss!" she sputtered. "Don't you have any manners? When

your aunt's ghost gets tangled in chains, you *help* her!"

Eden leaped up and tried to pull them off. She nudged Chuzzlewit for help, but he just yawned and stretched out on the bed to watch. When Marie was untangled, Eden helped her up.

"Much better," said Aunt Marie. "Child, walk with me."

She took Eden's arm, and the chains wrapped around a standing, full-length mirror. It nearly toppled, and Chuzzlewit meowed in alarm. But Eden caught the mirror just in time and righted it. She took her aunt's arm, and tried to pull the chains off her.

"No, Eden," said Aunt Marie, her tone softening. "These don't come off. They're chains of selfishness."

Eden tilted her head. "Selfishness?" she said. "But you said selfishness was good!"

Aunt Marie smiled weakly. "I was wrong," her aunt said. "Forget everything I told you. Oh, Eden!" Her aunt reached for a hug, but Eden pulled away. Aunt Marie landed on the floor with a thump.

"You're not my Aunt Marie," said Eden. "You're not even a ghost at all."

Aunt Marie sighed. "Not a ghost?" she asked. "I'm floating two feet off the ground! How much ghostlier do you want me to be?"

Eden nodded at Chuzzlewit, who started climbing up the canopy bed. Eden picked up a frilly parasol and swung it first over the ghost's head and below her feet.

"So what's holding you up, wires?" asked Eden. "Whatever it is, it's a good trick."

"The impertinence!" cried Aunt Marie. "This is the last time I visit *you* from the beyond."

"The real Aunt Marie would never say she was wrong," said Eden. "She raised me perfectly — to be a star."

"I've raised you to be a selfish ninny. But now I have the chance to make it right. I'm sending you three spirits tonight," said her aunt. "If you're lucky, they'll help you change your life . . . before you end up like me." Aunt Marie lifted her arms to show the chains.

"Now!" Eden cried.

Chuzzlewit leaped down off the canopy and landed on Aunt Marie. He took the fabric with him, trapping the older woman under the silk. Eden jumped on the canopy to wrestle with the body underneath. But when she pulled up the fabric, there was no one there, just Chuzzlewit. The fabric fell around his face like a bonnet. "How strange . . ." said Eden before settling back into her bed and falling asleep.

Later that night, Eden felt something fuzzy rubbing against her cheek. "It's not morning yet, Chuzzlewit," said Eden drowsily. Opening her eyes, she saw a young woman in a flowing white frock with flowers and ribbons in her hair. Sparkles flew from her fingertips.

"I'm the Spirit of Christmas Past," announced the girl. "Didn't your aunt tell you I was coming?" The girl waved her magic wand and Chuzzlewit floated up into her arms, leaving a trail of sparkles in the air behind him. The cat took off his sleep mask to find himself in midair! He

meowed in shock, and the spirit cuddled
him tight.

"The woogee woogee baby!" cooed the
spirit. She rubbed Chuzzlewit's nose with
hers. "I'm going to squish squish squish!"

Chuzzlewit struggled to get free. Nuzzling
the spirit was much worse than floating in
midair.

"Is this another nightmare?" asked Eden.

"No, silly!" said the spirit. "I've come to take you . . . hmm . . . now where did I put that note?"

The girl put down Chuzzlewit, who scurried under the bed. She emptied her pockets, tossing things into the air — a handful of sparkles, a pinch of snow, a blizzard of feathers. She examined something that looked like cotton candy.

"We're going to your girlhood Christmas," said the spirit finally. "What fun!"

Eden looked at the floor, sadly.

"I'm not sure that's such a good idea," she said.

Chapter 3

The spirit waved her wand, and a magic portal opened up. It pulled Eden and Chuzzlewit into a path of swirling colors.

The spirit grabbed Eden's hand and waved her wand. *"Pip-piddloo and don't be slow, it's off to your Christmas past we go!"* she chanted.

Suddenly, a magical portal opened up in the bedroom, and the spirit led Eden into it. Chuzzlewit leaped out from under the bed and pounced on Eden's nightgown from behind.

Eden turned to him. "Chuzzlewit?" she asked. The cat shook his head to tell Eden not to go, but the spirit misunderstood.

"Aww, kitty-witty's afraid we're not going to take him," she said. "Come on, kitty-witty, it's okay." The spirit pulled Eden into the portal. Chuzzlewit dug his claws into the floor, trying to hold Eden back. But the force of the portal dragged him in, too.

"*WHOOOOOOAH!*" cried Eden, clutching the cat.

Colors swirled all around them. Chuzzlewit's hair stood on end, as he climbed up Eden's dress into her free arm. He shut his eyes tight. Eden held the spirit's hand and enjoyed the rush of air as they traveled through time.

"I have to tell you," said the spirit. "I'm a *huge* fan of yours. Is it odd for you to hear that?"

Eden looked around at the tunnel of swirling color. "Uh, *that's* not the part that's odd for me. . . ." said Eden.

With a *whoosh*, they were dropped into the kitchen of a cold, bare house. Aunt Marie was seated at the table. Across from her, a twelve-year-old girl sat eating a crust of bread. Chuzzlewit opened his eyes and hopped to the ground where he resumed his snooty attitude.

"That's me," said Eden. "When I was younger."

The Spirit of Christmas Past looked

puzzled. "Something isn't right," she said. "We were supposed to be here at Christmas . . ."

"No," said Eden. "This is right."

"It can't be," said the spirit. "There is no tree, no stockings, no decorations. . . ." She put her arm around Eden. "You poor thing."

Eden swallowed. Chuzzlewit had sneakily climbed onto the table, unnoticed by Aunt Marie or young Eden. He crouched down low and pounced on young Eden's plate. To his dismay, he slid right through it, landing on the floor with a loud thump.

The spirit picked up Chuzzlewit and nuzzled him. "We can't touch food when we travel to other times, kitty-witty," she explained. "And no one can see or hear us. *Smoooch!*" She planted a huge, wet kiss on him. Chuzzlewit was horrified and struggled to escape the spirit's grasp.

Eden watched her younger self with her Aunt Marie.

"Can I go over to the Beadnells' house?" young Eden asked.

"Of course not," said Aunt Marie. "After dinner, we rehearse."

"I know," said young Eden. "But it's Christmas. . . ."

Aunt Marie looked at her, unmoved. "What about your future?" asked the older woman. "Don't you want to be a star?"

Eden nodded.

"Then use your time selfishly," said Aunt Marie. "In a selfish world, only the selfish succeed. Go work on your scales."

Young Eden slumped off to her room.

"Wait," said Kelly. "Aunt Marie made Eden work on *Christmas*?!"

"Well, every day," Barbie said. "But yes, on Christmas, too."

"That's not fair!" Kelly protested.

"It's not," Barbie agreed. "But — before, you said Eden was mean."

"I did . . . but . . ." Kelly fumbled.

Barbie put down the globe. "Maybe it's tougher to judge when you know the whole story," she said.

Kelly was silent a moment. "Maybe," she said. "Tell me what happened next."

Barbie picked up the snow globe. "So Eden stayed in her room and practiced her scales. . . ."

❄ ❄ ❄

In another room, Aunt Marie was asleep on the couch. Young Eden tiptoed to a window and snuck outside. Then she zoomed away on a sled — with the spirit, Eden, and Chuzzlewit floating beside her.

"Wheeeee!" yelled the spirit. "This is so much fun! Did you do this all the time?" Eden smiled, remembering. "As often as I could," she said.

The sled stopped at a large, beautiful house at the bottom of the hill. Young Eden raced to the door. It was opened by nine-year-old Catherine, who screamed with delight.

"Eden!" shouted young Catherine. "You made it!" She pulled her friend inside.

Eden smiled, watching her younger self. "Oh," she said. "This was my favorite place in the world!" The Beadnell house glowed with wreaths, garlands, and candles.

Next to the fireplace was a twinkling Christmas tree. A round table held a fragrant ham, a pot of steaming cider, cake, and cookies.

"I remember . . ." began Eden as she leaned back on the closed front door and fell right through! Eden collapsed in a heap in the foyer.

The spirit leaned over sympathetically. "That looked like it hurt," she said.

"Of course it hurt!" said Eden. "I fell through a wall!"

"Did I forget to mention we *float* through walls?" asked the spirit. "Oopsie."

The spirit grabbed Eden's arm to help her up. As she took in the festive surroundings, she gasped, and dropped Eden back onto the floor.

"Ouch!" said Eden. But the spirit's eyes were fixed on the enchanting scene in front of her. "A party!" she said, thrilled.

Eden sighed and pushed herself back up. She smelled freshly baked gingerbread and gazed at the stockings above the hearth. "They always put up a stocking for me," she said. "And gave me a bunch of presents."

Mrs. Beadnell came out to the living room with a wooden spoon in her hand. "Eden, will you taste the cookie batter?" she asked. "After all, snickerdoodles *are* your favorite."

Boz, the Beadnells' small black terrier, spotted Chuzzlewit. He made a leap for him, and Chuzzlewit scampered away. With a howl, the cat jumped onto Eden's face. She struggled to pry him off.

"Chuzzlewit!" she scolded. Turning to

the spirit, she said, "I thought you said they couldn't see us."

"People can't," explained the spirit. "But animals are more sensitive."

Mrs. Beadnell came over to soothe the terrier. "Boz, there's nothing there!" she said. "No more barking at shadows or we'll put you outside." Chuzzlewit heard this and happily slid down Eden. He stood directly in front of Boz and beamed wickedly.

Young Catherine pulled her friend over to the tree. She handed Eden a present wrapped in silver paper with a red ribbon and a sprig of holly tied to it. "For you," she said.

Young Eden tore the paper off and pulled out a snow globe. On the bottom was a music box, which played "O Christmas Tree."

Eden's eyes filled with tears. "You sing that song so beautifully," Catherine said. "It made me think of you."

"I love it," said young Eden. She was overwhelmed. "But I couldn't bring a gift for you. . . ."

Catherine waved her hand. "You're here. That's what's important!" The two friends smiled and hugged each other before running off toward young Catherine's bedroom.

Meanwhile, Chuzzlewit snuck off to the dining room and hopped on the back of a chair overlooking a table full of delicious Christmas cakes and cookies. He crouched down low, pretending to be ready to pounce to tease the dog. Boz noticed him and started barking loudly.

"Boz!" cried Mrs. Beadnell, running

over to him. "That's it, out of the house with you!" As she dragged Boz outside, Chuzzlewit laughed.

Young Eden and young Catherine reappeared wearing handmade Christmas costumes. "Time for the show, everyone!" Catherine announced.

The family gathered around excitedly. Young Catherine and young Eden sang "Jolly Old Saint Nicholas" and danced. Everyone shouted and whistled.

The girls finished with a fabulous pose, and the room exploded with applause. Everyone rushed to hug them. "That was amazing," said the spirit. "You said you didn't bring gifts. But you gave your talent. Look how happy it made everyone."

"I never thought of it that way," said Eden.

They were interrupted by a loud knock on the door. Eden's face went white. She picked up Chuzzlewit and grabbed the spirit's arm.

"Take me home," said Eden fiercely. "*Now.*"

Chapter 4

Mrs. Beadnell opened the door to find a very angry Aunt Marie.

"Where . . . is . . . Eden?" she spat out.

Eden buried her face in the spirit's shoulder. "That was my last Christmas there," said Eden sadly. "Aunt Marie never left me alone after that." The spirit was sympathetic. With a wave of her wand, the three of them landed back in Eden's bedroom.

Eden crawled into bed and pulled up the

covers next to Chuzzlewit. The spirit sat in front of Eden, trying to comfort her. Only Chuzzlewit was unconcerned. He lowered his sleeping mask, and curled up to go to sleep.

The spirit took Eden's hand. "I'm sorry," she said. Her touch snapped Eden back to reality.

"Don't be," said Eden, pulling away. "Aunt Marie was right. Those pageants were a waste of time." The spirit continued to look at Eden sympathetically. "Don't you have some place to go?" asked Eden. "You're not even real, anyway." She pulled her sleep mask over her eyes, and the spirit disappeared in a flash of sparkles.

Eden lifted her mask and peeked out. "Spirit?" she asked. But she had already gone. She slid down under the covers and

lowered her mask. Chuzzlewit lowered his mask, too. But he raised his mask once more time, just to make sure she was gone.

Later, Eden awoke to the sound of music, clapping, and laughing. Her room was filled with Christmas garlands, flowers, and candles. Musical instruments floated in the air. A jolly woman in a green dress sat in Eden's armchair, clapping to the music.

She watched gleefully as Eden's parasol and hat rack danced together in midair.

"Chuzzlewit," Eden whispered, but the cat was sleeping. The woman's green velvet dress was covered with toys, glitter, and garlands. She looked like a walking, talking Christmas tree. She waved her scepter, and Eden was pulled onto to her feet.

"Who are you?" Eden demanded. "What are you doing in my room?"

"Why, I'm celebrating," said the woman. "It's Christmas!" She pointed her scepter at the trumpet, which floated over to Chuzzlewit. With a blast, it played a loud wake-up fanfare in his ear.

"*ROWR!*" cried Chuzzlewit, waking in a flash. He leaped to the top of the canopy, hanging upside down by his claws.

The woman looked up at Chuzzlewit.

"Was that a little loud?" she asked. "I'm sorry. Now come join the party!" She waved her scepter, and Chuzzlewit floated upside-down until he hit the floor with a thump. Looking up, he noticed a red ribbon attached to her dress and started chasing after it.

"I am the Spirit of Christmas Present," the woman declared. "And I never come empty-handed." She handed Eden a present in shiny green-and-silver paper. Eden untied the red satin bow, and saw noisemakers, pointy hats, streamers, confetti, and a lovely iced cake inside. The hats landed on the heads of the spirit, Eden, and Chuzzlewit.

"It's a party in a box!" said the spirit.

The spirit looked at the hats and cake. "I think my Christmas party got mixed up with my birthday party," she said, frowning at her scepter. "Might be time to take this in for a tune-up." She waved it again and called to the instruments: "A little traveling music, please."

The floating trumpet, clarinet, and violin swung into a lively melody. The spirit twirled Eden around in a crazy dance. A portal opened, and Eden and the spirit danced into it. Tangled in red ribbon, Chuzzlewit hung from the spirit's dress like a decoration.

Once again, they were sucked into a tunnel of swirling color, then dumped out in the backstage of the Gadshill. The room was now bare, but the troupe was still there.

"How dare you drag me off?" Eden asked the spirit, smoothing her rumpled clothes. "Don't you know who I *am*?"

The spirit didn't answer. She was busy clapping to accordion music, played by Ann and Nan. Maurice was doing a complicated juggling act. Freddy was standing nearby, pulling tomatoes out of his hat and handing them to Maurice.

"Wait," Eden said, confused. "You said we were going to Christmas *present*, right?"

The spirit nodded. "So this is tomorrow," said Eden, sitting on a box. "Everyone's working. And they're happy! It isn't such a hardship at all!"

"You want us to work through Christmas, Eden?" Maurice asked. Eden turned, but realized Maurice wasn't talking to her.

Without missing a beat, Maurice threw a tomato at a poster of Eden. The tomato made a loud *SPLAT* and slid down the wall.

"Ow!" Maurice said. "That must have hurt."

Everyone laughed, including the Spirit. Eden turned on her angrily, but Maurice kept going. He threw more tomatoes: *SPLAT! SPLAT! SPLAT! SPLAT! SPLAT!*

Eden jumped to her feet. "You're all out of my theatre!" she screamed. The spirit

was still laughing. "Oh, that's priceless," she exclaimed, wiping her eyes.

"Priceless?" yelled Eden. "He's throwing tomatoes at me!"

"While juggling," said the spirit. "He's so talented. Put that in your act."

Eden was furious. "Whose side are you on?" she demanded. "These people wouldn't be anywhere without me!"

Freddy looked around nervously. "We'd better clean up before Catherine gets back," he said. "I don't think she'd like us throwing tomatoes at her friend."

Just then, Catherine came in, carrying a large sack. The troupe fumbled around, trying to hide the tomatoes.

"Hello, everyone!" said Catherine. "Did you miss —"

Then she spotted the huge tomato stain on the poster. She put down her sack and looked at everyone with a raised eyebrow. Freddy was sick to his stomach.

"We're sorry —" he began.

Eden waited eagerly. Catherine would never let them get away with this.

Chapter 5

Catherine said nothing. With a serious look on her face, she walked over to Maurice and held her hand out. Guiltily, he handed over a tomato. Catherine held it for a moment.

With all her strength, she hurled it at the poster.

SPLAT!

It hit a perfect bull's-eye. Everyone cheered wildly. Ann and Nan picked up their accordions, and Maurice resumed throwing tomatoes. Catherine extended an arm to Freddy. "Shall we dance?" she asked. He was thrilled.

Eden couldn't believe what she was seeing. She thought Catherine was her *friend* — why would she turn on her like this? She stormed over to the spirit. "I want to leave," she said. "Now."

The spirit stopped clapping. "Right *now*?" she asked, disappointed. Eden nodded, and the spirit sighed. She grabbed Eden's arm and they entered the swirling portal. At the last second, Chuzzlewit leaped onto the back of the spirit's dress.

The portal spilled the three of them onto a London street. "This isn't my bedroom," Eden said, looking around. "I told you to take me home."

"I thought you said you just wanted to leave," said the spirit. "You have to be more specific." She scratched her backside. "Did I sit in something?" she asked. She reached behind and pulled Chuzzlewit off her dress.

The cat howled unhappily as the spirit held him by his neck. "Feisty thing, aren't you?" she asked. The moment she put him down, he raced off straight into the path of two horses. The horses reared up and whinnied loudly, while a couple of women tried to calm them down.

Eden realized she was standing next to Catherine and Catherine's sister, Nell. Catherine's horse had a large sack on the back, while Nell's horse was attached to a carriage.

"She's a monster, if you ask me," said

Nell. "To keep you away from your family after everything we did for her . . ."

Catherine shook her head. "She's not a monster," she said. "I can get mad at her, but I can't hate her." Catherine looked at her watch. "I've got to hurry, or I'll be late for my other show."

Eden had been sympathetic up to that point. "Other show?!" she screamed. "I knew it! You're done at the Gadshill! *DONE!*"

"Another show!" said the spirit. "I hope we can get a seat!"

They followed Catherine to a gritty street in a poor part of town. The crumbling buildings were black with soot, and garbage lined the curb. Chuzzlewit made a face, not wanting to get his paws dirty. He jumped into Eden's arms.

"She picked this place because it was out of the way," said Eden. "She didn't want me to find out about it! Devious!"

Eden shouted at Catherine as she took down a sack from her horse. "What new actress is waiting for you?" taunted Eden as Catherine entered a grim courtyard. "Anastasia Warbler? Renata Trillby? Cassand —"

A little boy in a torn scarf and rags came up to greet Catherine. "Catherine!" he shouted. A crowd of children poured into the courtyard, talking happily and cheering. Most of them had dirty faces and were dressed in tattered clothes.

An older man in a patched coat came out to greet Catherine. Her face lit up when the children gathered around her. "Hi, everyone!" she said.

The boy in the scarf clapped his hands excitedly. "Merry Christmas, Catherine!" a girl in a ragged dress limped over. "Merry Christmas, Catherine," she said shyly. Catherine put her sack down and gave the girl a hug. "Merry Christmas, Tammy," she said.

The other children piled on to hug Catherine, too. "All right," said Catherine, laughing. "Big group hug." The spirit came over and pushed up Eden's chin.

"You're right," joked the spirit. "She *is* devious."

Chapter 6

Catherine looked at the children. "Is everyone ready for Christmas costumes?" she asked. "I have one for everybody." She reached into her bag and handed them out one by one.

The kids squealed with delight. Catherine took out a silvery angel dress and a pointy elf hat. Tammy tugged Catherine's sleeve. "Did you tell Eden Starling about us?" she asked. "Will she come to our show?"

The children began jumping up and down. "Yes, will she?" they asked. A shadow crossed Catherine's face, and she leaned down to Tammy.

"I did tell Eden about you," said Catherine. "And she wanted me to tell you she's very sorry she can't come, but she personally wishes each of you a merry Christmas."

The kids looked at one another and beamed. One kid said to another, "Hear that? Eden Starling wishes *me* a merry Christmas."

Tammy looked at Catherine. "It must be amazing to hear her sing," she said. "You're so lucky."

"I am lucky," agreed Catherine. "Because I get to hear *you* sing! Now come on. Time to put on costumes for the show!"

Barbie turned away from the snow globe. "Eden was amazed by the way the children came alive with Catherine," she told Kelly. "It wasn't just the new clothes. It was Catherine's attention . . . the simple fact that she cared."

While the children sang onstage, the man in the patched coat came over to

Catherine. "Thank you for this," he said. "You've done so much for our orphanage."

Catherine waved her hand. "It's the least I can do," she said. In a low voice, she asked, "Have you heard any more about the closing?"

"Only rumors," he said.

"What closing?" Eden asked the spirit.

"The orphanage doesn't have the funds to stay open," said the spirit. "They'll probably close before spring."

Eden looked at Tammy's smiling face. "What will happen to the children?" she asked.

The spirit smoothed her crazy dress. "They'll become street urchins, I suppose," she said. "But that's all humbug to you . . . right?"

Eden swallowed. When the song was over, she burst into applause with the rest of the audience. Chuzzlewit woke up, annoyed.

Catherine walked up to the children. "That was amazing!" she said. "I'll see you all very soon!" The kids' smiles faded.

"No!" said the boy in the scarf.

"Don't go!" said someone else.

Tammy threw her arms around Catherine. "Can't you just stay longer?" she begged. "Please?"

Catherine smiled. "I'd love to, but . . ." she said. "I have to go to work."

Eden joined the kids in shouting, "No!"

The spirit turned to Eden. "Have you changed your mind about working through Christmas?" she asked.

Eden lifted her chin. "Not at all," she

said. "I'm just saying she could take a slightly longer break. *Slightly*." The spirit looked doubtful.

They were interrupted by a loud ringing noise. The spirit pulled an alarm clock off her dress. "Would you look at the time!" she said. "I'm late. Take my sleeve. . . ."

Eden was disappointed. "*Now?*" she asked.

"Surely you need your beauty sleep," the spirit said. "What was it your aunt said . . . ?" She tapped her forehead.

"'In a selfish world, only the selfish succeed,'" said Eden softly. She picked up Chuzzlewit, looking back at the children. "All right," she said slowly. "Let's go."

Chapter 7

Later that night, Chuzzlewit felt a hand on his face. A beautiful woman was standing at the foot of the bed. She wore a soft, red velvet gown and a hooded cape. In one hand she held a scepter with a snowy crystal ball.

The woman raised her finger to her mouth, as if to say, "*Shhhh.*" She floated to Eden's side of the bed and smoothed her hair. Eden opened her eyes and saw a lovely, wise face.

"Hello," said Eden. "You're the third spirit, aren't you?"

The woman nodded. "The Spirit of Christmas Future. Are you ready to come with me?"

Eden sat up in bed. "I don't know," she said. "Will I like what I see?"

"You might not," admitted the spirit. "But we need to face things that frighten us.

That's how we grow." She took Eden's hand, while Chuzzlewit tried to hide under the covers. The spirit smiled and picked him up. "Ready?" she asked.

Eden took a deep breath and nodded. The spirit banged her scepter on the ground, and a portal opened up. They walked through the swirling colors together.

Unlike other portals, this one had holes in it. "Every choice you make alters what will happen," explained the spirit. She led them to the largest hole. "We'll find your most likely future right here."

A cold wind blew in the tunnel. Eden shivered, and Chuzzlewit crawled into the spirit's robes. "It's so cold," Eden complained.

"This future starts with a cold choice,"

said the spirit. "You made everyone work on Christmas. When you found out they came late, you fired them."

Eden lifted her chin. "I warned them that would happen."

The spirit agreed, "Yes, you did. Unfortunately, their replacements didn't work out so well. Like the hypnotist . . ."

❄ ❄ ❄

They looked up at a screen on the wall of the portal. It showed a hypnotist dangling a watch in front of Eden.

"And when you hear the word *Brava*," he said, "you'll cluck like a chicken!"

Another screen showed Eden finishing a song to loud applause. "*Brava! Brava!*" the audience shouted. But when she opened her mouth to sing, Eden clucked like a chicken. She tried to correct herself, but she only clucked more and more.

Chuzzlewit giggled, until Eden glared at him. The spirit led them a few feet farther down the portal. "And the trained dogs . . ." said the spirit, pointing to another screen.

In this scene, Eden stood in a spotlight. Chuzzlewit raced onstage, followed by four barking dogs in tuxedos. Chuzzlewit dived into Eden's skirt to hide, and the stampeding dogs trampled them both.

Eden turned away from the screen. "Enough!" she cried. "So what if that happened? My fans would stand by me."

"Then you have nothing to fear," said the spirit as she pulled them into the portal. They were spilled out into a messy, broken-down home. "What's this?" asked Eden, disgusted by the dirty floor and torn curtains.

A voice came from another room. "Get him, Chuzzlewit!" It was her future self, Eden realized. A mouse ran inside, chased by the future Chuzzlewit. The cat had barely any fur and no fancy collar. Chuzzlewit was horrified, and he checked his plump, white paw to make sure he didn't look like that.

The future Eden ran after her cat. The future Eden was still beautiful, but her clothes were tattered. Eden gasped.

"Is that . . ." she sputtered, "*ME?*"

Future Chuzzlewit leaped on the mouse but missed. Future Eden sank down on a couch full of holes. A rusty spring poked through the fabric.

"I'm sorry, Chuzzlewit," said future Eden. "That would have been your Christmas dinner."

Eden was furious. "Is this a joke?" she asked the spirit. "This *can't* be my future!"

Chapter 8

The spirit tapped her scepter on the floor of future Eden's house, making a swirl of sparkles. A gust of wind hit the window, making future Eden shiver. "Too cold," she said, rising to close the window. But there was a piece of paper against the glass.

Future Eden looked at the paper. "'Catherine Beadnell Presents Spring Fashions,'" she read. "'Come to her studio in Grindstone Square to see work from

Europe's most famous designer.'" Eden sat on the windowsill and hugged her torn sweater. "I haven't seen her in . . ." she said.

Eden jumped up. "What?!?" she shouted at her future self. "She can *help*. Catherine would never let you live like this!"

"Grindstone Square?" said future Eden. "But she wouldn't be there today. It's Christmas."

"*Do it!*" Eden commanded her future self. "Go to the studio and see her!"

"Let's follow them," said future Eden, picking up Chuzzlewit.

The spirit looked at her carefully. "Are you sure?" she asked.

"Of course!" said Eden, closing her eyes. The spirit took Eden's arm.

❄ ❄ ❄

Catherine's studio was large and elegant, on a fashionable London street. A roomful of seamstresses were hard at work. When Eden and future Eden saw Catherine, they both gasped, "There she is!"

Future Catherine looked glamorous. Her hair was done in beautiful ringlets, and she wore a striped silk dress. "Holiday?!" she yelled at someone. "Who said anything about a *holiday*? If *I* have to work, *you* have to work."

The seamstress's eyes filled with tears. "But it's Christmas!" she cried.

"I know," snapped future Catherine. "That means there are only two weeks before we show the new line."

Eden was puzzled. "She doesn't sound like Catherine," she said. "She sounds like . . ."

Future Catherine looked up and saw future Eden at the door. "*Eden!*" she shouted.

Future Catherine ran to hug future Eden. She bent down to scratch future Chuzzlewit's scrawny chin. "Hi, Chuzzie," she said. Chuzzlewit, of course, made a face.

"I can't believe you're here on Christmas," she said. "I thought you went home to your family."

Catherine shook her head. "I don't celebrate Christmas anymore," she said. "I soured on the holiday when . . ." She pretended to forget. "When was it again? Oh, yes! When you *fired* me because I came in late on Christmas Day!"

Future Eden stuttered. "Right. Um . . ."

Future Catherine picked up a bolt of fabric. "It's okay," she said. "You did me a favor. You proved me wrong."

Eden knew what was coming next. "No . . . don't say it, Catherine. Don't say it. . . ." she pleaded.

"It *is* a selfish world. And in a selfish world, only the selfish succeed," said Catherine, unrolling the fabric.

Future Eden paused. "I'm not . . . a hundred percent sure that's true. . . ."

"Oh, I am," said Catherine. "I tried to be selfless. I looked out for everyone at the Gadshill. I tried to help the orphanage. Do you know what happened?" She turned to future Eden angrily.

"I fired you," said future Eden softly.

"I couldn't find work," said Catherine. "I had to take a job out of town. Know what I found when I got back?"

Future Eden shook her head.

"Nothing," she said. "The orphanage

had closed. I had no idea. There was one girl I was ready to take in myself . . . and she was gone. They all were. Out in the world, fending for themselves . . ." Catherine's voice got shaky, and Eden felt sick to her stomach.

"No . . ." future Eden said. "Not the children . . . oh, Catherine . . ."

Chapter 9

Eden moved to comfort Catherine, forgetting her friend couldn't see her.

"I learned my lesson," Catherine said. "Caring hurt, so I stopped. Now I just concentrate on myself. I'm a star — just like you were."

Eden went up to her friend. "Catherine," she begged, "don't make the same mistakes I made. You're better than that. Don't be like me. Do you hear me, Catherine?"

But of course, her friend couldn't hear her.

Future Eden now knew that Catherine couldn't help her, but she forced herself to ask. Her friend shook her head. "I'm done helping people, Eden," she said. "It never works."

"I'm sorry I bothered you," said future Eden. She opened the door to the studio

and looked back. "Merry Christmas, Catherine," she said, meaning it.

A few seconds later, future Eden was back on the snowy streets of London. The spirit, Eden, and Chuzzlewit followed behind. Before future Catherine closed the door, she grabbed an old scarf and tossed it to Eden. "Here," she yelled. "It's cold out."

The wind blew the scarf over future Eden's head. She dived after it, landing in a snowdrift. The old scarf was sopping wet. "It's useless," announced future Eden. "Just our luck, Chuzzlewit!"

But the cat wasn't around. Future Eden heard a tapping sound and looked up at Catherine's studio. Future Chuzzlewit was in the window, snuggled happily on a pile of fabric.

The cat stretched his paws and waved. Just as he was about to go to sleep, Catherine grabbed him by the neck. She threw future Chuzzlewit out the door and into the cold snow. Without missing a beat the cat got up, dusted itself off, and made a beeline for future Eden. He looked up to her with his big, brown eyes and purred, as if to say "You know you still love me." And he was right. How could she resist?

"How did we come to this, Chuzzlewit?" asked future Eden, sighing. "I wish . . . oh, it doesn't matter. Come on."

Eden watched her future self trudge through the snow. She was stunned by what she had just seen. The spirit put a comforting arm around her.

"No! This can't be my life!" cried Eden. "There *has* to be a way to change things!"

The Spirit of Christmas Future shook her head. "That chance passed long ago," she said. "As of now, this is your future."

Eden buried her face in her hands. "But it can't be! It's too horrible. I don't want to live this life. I want to change." She got down on her knees and pleaded with the spirit.

"Please, please give me another chance!" she begged.

The spirit didn't say anything. But she picked up Chuzzlewit, pulled Eden close and stepped into the portal.

Chapter 10

Eden awoke from sleep with a gasp. "Please!" she said, looking around the room. Her fancy covers were rumpled, and her eyemask had been torn off. Chuzzlewit was happily curled on the pillow.

"I'm home . . . in my room," Eden assured herself. "Is anyone else here?!" She looked around the room. "No, it's just us. It's over," she said.

Sun streamed through the window. Eden leaped out of bed and pulled back the sheer curtains. Outside, the quaint streets were decorated for Christmas. Doors were covered in wreaths, and Christmas trees peeked through every window. Snowflakes drifted from the sky.

"It's Christmas morning!" Eden realized with delight. "It hasn't happened yet!"

She scooped up Chuzzlewit and whirled him around in a giddy dance. They got tangled in the long canopy curtain hanging down from the bed. Edith looked in Chuzzlewit's eyes.

"The portals, Chuzzlewit!" she cried. "Those portals to the future — we can choose a new one! We don't have to make the same mistakes!" Then another thought occurred to her. "We can make this the best Christmas *ever*! Isn't it wonderful?"

The cat yawned.

"We have to go shopping!" Eden exclaimed, jumping up. She rushed to the door, and stopped. "It's Christmas," she realized. "The stores are all closed. Chuzzlewit, what do we do?" As she ran toward him, she tripped on the canopy. *CRASH!* She fell to the floor and looked up at Chuzzlewit. They both burst out in laughter.

She looked around the room, and her face lit up. "I know," said Eden. "I'm rich! We'll go shopping here!"

Leaping up, she raced to the closet. She pulled out the largest bag she could find. Inside it, she put a small velvet bag. "Come on, Chuzzlewit!" she said. "Let's go Christmas shopping!"

The cat watched dizzily as Eden zoomed around the house, throwing things in her

bag. He curled up to go to sleep, until Eden scooped him up.

Over at the Gadshill, the troupe was preparing for rehearsal. Maurice was riding his unicycle and juggling. Ann and Nan danced together in matching outfits. Freddy was practicing a trick with colored handkerchiefs.

Eden burst in the door in a rush of

excitement. She wore a red cap with white trim, and she carried a large sack. "Stop!" she shouted. "Stop rehearsing! Stop everything!"

Ann and Nan gasped. Maurice bumped into a wall and fell off his unicycle. Freddy dropped his hat, and a white rabbit hopped out. The performers shook with fear.

"Please don't fire us," begged Freddy. "We're all here. Okay, maybe we were a couple minutes late, but —"

Ann and Nan got down on their knees.

"Please let us . . ." said Ann.

". . . keep our jobs!" finished Nan.

Eden waved her hands. "It's okay!" she said. "I'm not here to fire anyone! It's Christmas! I'm here to send you home to your families!"

Everyone stared at her.

"But you said . . ." began Maurice.

"Forget what I said," commanded Eden. "I was wrong." She motioned toward the door. "Go! Go!"

The performers looked at one another and smiled slowly. It was too good to be true.

"Wait," Eden said as they started to leave. "I have presents! And look!"

Eden pushed Chuzzlewit forward. The howling cat was dressed in an elf suit. He looked *very* unhappy.

"A little elf to help me," she explained. "I saved my shopping for the last minute, and everything's closed today." Eden put down her bag and rummaged through it. "I just grabbed what I had . . . Merry Christmas!" she said.

She handed Maurice a bowl, and Ann a cuckoo clock. Nan received a nutcracker, and she tossed Freddy a globe. The troupe looked at the pile of strange gifts. "Thanks, Eden," they mumbled.

"Catherine, I'm saving yours for later," said Eden. She was too excited to notice everyone's puzzled looks. "Wait — there's more!" said Eden. "I found something I wanted to give you."

She reached into the bag and pulled out sacks of coins tied with red ribbon. They jiggled as she handed them to Maurice, Ann, Nan, Freddy, and Catherine.

"Christmas bonuses!" she said. "Because you're all so talented, and it is truly an honor to work with you. Now go have a holiday," she said. "I'll see you in two weeks when we open! Merry Christmas!"

Everyone was stunned. They gathered around to thank her.

Freddy came up to her first. "Thank you," he said. He fluttered his hand and produced . . . a bouquet of carrots. His face fell. "It was supposed to be flowers," he explained.

"I love them," Eden said sincerely. In a low voice, she asked, "But I have a favor to ask." She handed Freddy an envelope. He looked puzzled. As he stepped aside to read it, Ann and Nan came up to Eden.

The girls did a tap dance and sang "Merry Christmas." Eden hugged them both. "That was beautiful," she said. "Thank you."

Maurice approached, holding his sack of coins. "I was wrong about you, Eden," he said. "You're one of the good ones. *Merci*." He kissed her on each cheek.

Freddy finished reading Eden's note. "Yes!" he said excitedly. He took Eden's hands. "*YES!*" he said again. With a giddy look at Catherine, he raced out of the theatre. He kicked up his heels and clicked them.

Eden beamed. Catherine looked after

Freddy, confused. "What was that all about?" she asked.

"I guess he liked his present," Eden said mysteriously.

Catherine pointed at the presents. "Eden, I —" she began.

"I know you've been working on another show behind my back," said Eden, lifting her chin.

"Let me explain," said Catherine, worried.

"And I think it's *WONDERFUL!*" said Eden. "I want to go with you to see the kids perform. I understand I might have a couple of fans at the orphanage."

Catherine looked surprised. "You do, but . . . how do you know about the orphanage?" she asked.

Eden shrugged. "Maybe it came to me in

a dream," she said. "Come on — let's hurry!"

Catherine couldn't believe it. "Wait," she said. Catherine wrapped Eden's scarf around the bottom half of her face, and put up her hood. "Let's make our mystery guest a surprise."

She grabbed her sack of clothes for the children and they rushed out.

Chapter 11

In glittering costumes, the kids lit up the stage. Their singing filled the orphanage courtyard. Catherine watched them do their concert finale.

"*Joy to the world* . . ." the children sang.

Catherine checked to make sure Eden was in her hiding place. Outside the courtyard, Eden lowered her scarf and grinned. When the song ended, everyone stood up and clapped wildly.

"That was amazing, everyone," said Catherine. The kids beamed. "But we're not done. I've brought you a Christmas present. A special guest you might want to meet." Catherine called to someone offstage. "Special guest?"

Eden swept into the courtyard, lowering the hood of her cape. She whipped off her scarf and announced, "Merry Christmas, everybody!"

Everyone gasped.

"*Eden Starling?!*" said Tammy, in disbelief.

"Tammy?" Eden said. The young girl nearly toppled over.

"You know my name!" she cried, hobbling toward the star. Eden rushed to the stage and hugged her.

The boy in the scarf broke away. "I want a hug, too!" he said. Soon all the kids piled on Eden. She loved it.

"Catherine's told me so much about you, I feel like I know you," explained Eden. "Lizabeth, Jacob, Edmund . . . you were all incredible," she said. "I'm so happy to be part of your Christmas."

The kids buzzed around her, while Catherine wondered how Eden knew their names.

"I have a special present for you," Eden continued. "I am going to personally adopt this place." She turned to the orphanage head. "Anything you need — new furniture, toys, books . . . I'll make sure you have it. I want these children to have the best."

The man in the patched sweater rose up,

stunned. "Miss Starling," he said. "There are no words . . . thank you."

Tammy hugged Eden again. "This is the best Christmas ever!" she cried. Eden returned Tammy's hug.

As the kids continued to sing and celebrate, Catherine turned to her friend. "You're incredible," she said. "Where did all this come from?"

"You wouldn't believe me if I told you," said Eden. "It had a lot to do with you." She took Catherine's hand. "Thank you."

They hugged. "Thank *you*," Catherine said. "For giving me back my friend."

"Oh! Your Christmas present!" Eden exclaimed. "Part one."

Chuzzlewit was tired of Christmas. As he walked off to find a quiet spot to nap, he smelled something in Eden's sack. Cookies! Eden had baked them earlier, and put them in fancy tins. Chuzzlewit worked the lid off a tin to find a pile of sugary, decorated treats. He took a bite cautiously, not sure if his teeth would slide through the cookie. When he got a bite, he dived right in.

Eden took her friend's hand and led her through the courtyard, out to the street. Eden whistled, and a magnificent, horse-drawn carriage pulled up next to them.

"Eden . . ." Catherine began.

"They're the fastest horses money can buy," explained Eden. "If we leave now, we can make it to your parents' house in time for dinner. That is . . . if it's okay for me to tag along."

Catherine clapped her hands together. "Okay? I'd *love* if you came home with me."

A male voice interrupted them. "Ladies?"

Catherine and Eden looked up and saw Freddy jump down from the driver's seat. Catherine lit up. "Freddy!" she said. "You're driving us?"

"It would be my greatest honor," he said, taking off his top hat.

He reached out his hand to help Catherine into the carriage. Freddy looked at Eden, and she nodded. Freddy took a deep breath and pulled back his hand.

"But first, I have something to ask," he said. "Sometime when it's not Christmas, I was wondering . . ." Freddy wiped his forehead. "If I could have the pleasure . . . that is, if I could have the honor . . ."

"Freddy," said Catherine, "are you asking me on a date?"

Freddy looked at the ground. "Yes?"

Catherine smiled warmly. "I'd love it," she said. "Thank you." She kissed him on the cheek and climbed into the carriage.

Freddy leaped gleefully and kicked his heels. "Yes!" he cried.

"Thank you so much, Eden!" said Catherine. She was amazed by her friend's kindness.

Eden put up her hand. "Wait," she said. "There's more. Although, this is really *my* Christmas present." She pulled a snow globe out of the velvet bag. Catherine had given it to her when they were kids.

"You still have it!" exclaimed Catherine.

"I do," said Eden. "From now on, I'm

keeping it on my nightstand. That way, I'll remember to hold the feeling of Christmas in my heart every day. One day I'll pass it down to my children, grandchildren, and great-grandchildren . . . so they'll remember, too."

Catherine was touched. "Thank you," she said. "It's the perfect present."

"Hey, where's Chuzzlewit?" Eden asked, looking around the courtyard. A satisfied *BURP!* came from a corner bench. Chuzzlewit was stretched out on a pile of empty cookie tins. He had eaten every last cookie, and his white fur was streaked with colored frosting. "Oh, Chuzzie," Eden said, scooping him up.

She placed the cat beside her in the carriage. As it began to roll away, one of the wheels caught in the snow. "I'm afraid the carriage won't make it through this weather," said Freddy.

Eden and Catherine turned to each other in panic.

Eden looked at the snow globe in her hand. Inside, there were three dancing women — the spirits, she realized. The women waved their scepters together, making sparkles. The sparkles covered the carriage like falling snowflakes and swirled around it.

Freddy leaped off the carriage. "Did you see that?" he asked.

"I thought it was one of your magic tricks," said Catherine.

Freddy shook his head. "I've never seen anything like it," he said.

"I have," said Eden.

Freddy and Catherine looked at her, but Eden didn't say anything. All three spirits were singing "We Wish You a Merry Christmas." The sparkles faded away, and Catherine, Eden, and Freddy found themselves in a gorgeous Christmas sleigh.

"Amazing!" said Freddy.

"What?!" said Catherine. "How . . . ?"

The snow globe in Eden's hands was no longer moving. She smiled at the three spirits, grateful for their magic. The children followed Eden and Chuzzlewit out to the street. They waved and shouted good-bye as Freddy helped Eden into the sleigh.

"Good-bye! Merry Christmas!" Eden and Catherine called out. "We'll see you soon!"

The sleigh started down the street. Looking back, Eden saw a familiar face. Aunt Marie floated above the crowd, no longer in chains. She smiled and blew Eden a kiss. The sleigh drove into the distance, and Eden and Catherine continued to sing. . . .

Chapter 12

Kelly tugged her sister's sleeve. "And did they get to the Beadnells' in time for dinner?" she asked anxiously.

Barbie put the snow globe back on the shelf. "They did," she said. "And every year after that they spent Christmas the same way. They helped others in the morning and spent the evening together with their families and friends."

Kelly was silent for a moment. "Barbie?" she asked.

"Yes, sweetie?" answered her sister.

"That snow globe that Catherine gave Eden . . . the one that Eden said she'd pass down to her children . . ." Kelly pointed to the shelf. "Is that the same snow globe? Are we related to Eden? Did the story really happen?"

Barbie smiled mysteriously. "Maybe," she said. "But I do know one thing for

sure." She took the snow globe down and handed it to Kelly. "This is yours now."

Kelly clutched the glass ball in her hand. "Really? For keeps?"

Barbie nodded. "For keeps," she said. "So it can remind you to keep the beauty of Christmas in your heart every day of the year."

"Just like Eden," said Kelly, smiling. "Thanks, Barbie. Merry Christmas!"

Barbie put an arm around her sister. "Merry Christmas, Kel."

Inside the snow globe, the three spirits celebrated. They waved their scepters and disappeared into a sea of sparkles.

Barbie STARS IN HER FIRST-EVER HOLIDAY MOVIE!

Barbie

in A CHRISTMAS CAROL

On DVD
November
2008

www.Barbie.com/Christmas